"QUIETLY, WE ROSE"

A JOURNEY OF HOPE, HOME, AND HOLDING ON

DISHA Y BANGERA

Made with ♥ on the Notion Press Platform
www.notionpress.com

To my mother, whose love lit my darkest paths.

And to every soul who rose quietly, with courage,

through storms of their own.

Contents

Contents

Foreword

Some stories reach you with noise; others, with quiet power. *Quietly We Rose* is one such story it does not demand your attention, it earns it through sincerity, resilience, and raw humanity.

The journey is not made of perfect moments it is made of truth. In these pages, you'll walk beside her through dimly lit days and deeply felt love. You'll witness a woman navigating family responsibilities, financial hardship, emotional turbulence, and spiritual awakening all while holding on to grace and grit.

This book is more than a personal narrative it's a reminder of the quiet warriors among us. Those who rise not because life has been kind, but because they've chosen to believe in tomorrow. Through the ups and downs, you'll see a family who kept faith alive, a woman who found strength in motherhood and meaning in struggle, and a relationship that endured despite storms and silence.

As you turn these pages, you may find parts of your own journey echoing within hers. Let this story soften you, strengthen you, and remind you: the quietest rise can be the most powerful one.

Preface

Some stories begin with grand events.

Mine...began in silence in quiet sacrifices, whispered prayers, and the soft strength of a woman who kept walking, even when the road disappeared beneath her feet.

This book is not just a recollection of events—it's the reflection of a heart that broke, healed, and chose to love again. *Quietly We Rose* is the story of two people who stood by each other through life's storms: failed promises, crushing debts, heartbreaks, and long nights filled with unanswered questions.

It's a journey of a daughter who became a caregiver, a wife who became a warrior, and a mother who discovered her own soul while holding her family together. And somewhere in between pain and prayer, I found a path that led me to healing, peace, and purpose.

I've written these chapters not as a lesson, but as a mirror. Maybe you'll see a part of yourself here—in the struggle, in the hope, in the quiet strength we often forget we carry.

Because sometimes, the strongest people don't shout their victories. They rise quietly.

Disha *Y. Bangera*

Acknowledgements

First and foremost, I want to thank **my readers** each of you who chose to pick up this book, spend time with these pages, and step into the world I've lived and written about. Your time, your emotions, and your connection mean more than words can say.

To **my family**, thank you for walking every path with me, through the highs and the depths. Your presence has been my strength, and your love, my anchor. To my mother, whose blessings continue to guide me from beyond I carry you in every word I write.

To **my friends**, who stood by me without judgment, offering comfort, laughter, and encouragement in moments I didn't even realize I needed it thank you.

A special thanks to **Jenny**, who has been more than a friend; she's been my mirror, my support, and my witness. And lastly, to **life itself**, with all its unpredictable lessons, for teaching me how to survive, evolve, and quietly rise.

With gratitude,
Disha Y. Bangera

Through My Mother's Eyes

At the age of eight, I didn't really know what family meant. Emotions, bonds, responsibilities these were just words floating around me, not things I truly understood. Life felt like a blur. I didn't yet have the awareness to grasp what was happening around me, nor did I question it.

It wasn't until I reached my early teens, around the time I entered the tenth grade, that I started becoming aware. I began noticing the world around me and more importantly, my place in it. I struggled to make friends, often feeling like I wasn't good enough. That quiet voice of self-doubt kept whispering, making me feel small in classrooms filled with laughter and easy friendships.

That was also the year my father passed away. I was thirteen. And though it may sound strange even heartless to some I wasn't devastated. Somewhere deep inside, I had already felt a kind of distance. It wasn't that I didn't care, but rather, I had long learned to rely on someone else entirely my mother. She was the one who had carried the family, held us together, and played every role life demanded, quietly and without complaint.

My elder sister got married at a young age. My brother started working early. And while my father was physically present during some of those years, it was my mother who raised us in the truest sense. I say this without shame: my father couldn't carry the responsibilities of being a husband or father in the way life required. But my mother she gave it everything she had, and more.

There is one memory, small on the surface but unforgettable to me. It was during *Uttarayan*, the kite festival. That year, I remember noticing something quietly.

My mother had received a small portion of papdi flour someone from the neighborhood had given it to her. It wasn't much, but she was so happy. She made papdi out of it and fed it to us with love, her face glowing with joy. There was no hesitation, no ego only gratitude.

What stayed with me was not just that she cooked something special from a small gift, but the grace with which she received it. She never let pride come in the way of love. Our neighbors often shared food with us, even though she cooked for us every day. She welcomed everything with warmth. I never once saw her express envy, resentment, or shame. She accepted kindness with dignity and gave back tenfold in love, respect, and resilience.

Today, at this age, I understand her pain and strength in a way I couldn't back then. I see the sacrifices she made, the way she swallowed her emotions and carried her responsibilities as a wife, a mother, a daughter-in-law. She endured what many would've crumbled under. And yet, she stood tall not loud, not showy, but unshakably strong.

She has become my definition of what it means to be a woman. Graceful. Resilient. Humble. And deeply powerful.

CHAPTER TWO

School Days & the Samosa Stop

There was no single school I called mine I changed schools three times. The first two never gave me anything lasting no deep friendships, no emotional pull, no bonds. I was always there, present physically but never attached in heart. Maybe it was me, or maybe the time just wasn't ripe yet. I walked the corridors, sat in classrooms, but never belonged.

It all changed in my third school the one I chose not for academics, but for a simple reason: I wanted commerce, not science.

That's where I met Anish.

He wasn't loud. He didn't talk much. But he had something most people never do presence. Quiet, comforting, unwavering presence. He made me feel seen, understood... without needing to say a word.

He became my first real friend.

From that quiet companionship grew a circle of joy: Viral, Harsh, Anita, Saaransh, Rubeka, Jasmine, and many more. A group that made every single day a celebration of youth — careless laughter, harmless mischief, and a bond unburdened by expectations.

Anish would come to pick me up every single morning — a gesture he turned into a ritual. And our gang, always waiting, always cheerful, would start the day together. School wasn't about textbooks for us — it was about togetherness, about shared jokes, silly secrets, and spontaneous bursts of laughter in quiet corners.

And every afternoon, without fail, there was the samosa stop a tiny stall tucked away from the main road, where Anish and I would go after school. That place still exists. And whenever I visit that city, I go there — not just for the samosa, but to taste the memory, to feel the presence of a time that was so pure.

I don't know where most of those classmates are today. But after nearly seventeen years, Anish found his way back into my life like he never really left. One day, we spoke again, and the past rushed in like it was only yesterday.

I met him. After all those years.

Nothing had changed except the number of candles on our cakes. He was still not so talkative. And I was still... me. The one who would talk, and he would listen just like always.

He came to pick me up again this time, from the station. And just like that, those school memories came alive. Two grown adults now, a mother and a father, exchanging stories about life, family, careers but beneath the surface, something still softly flickered.

That unspoken space between us it still existed. Maybe it always will.

We are happy in our separate lives. Content, matured, fulfilled. But some corners of the heart never age. They remain untouched, unshaken holding on to something pure, innocent, un manipulated. That meeting reminded me: some bonds are beyond time.

Some friendships never need updates.
They simply pause and quietly continue.

CHAPTER THREE

Lessons of the Heart

After school, I chose to pursue my graduation. It wasn't easy. Financial hurdles and emotional exhaustion often ran side by side. From 12th grade through to my final year of college, every step forward was marked by silent battles — balancing studies, responsibilities at home, and the quiet longing for something just for myself.

It was during my first year of college that I met someone his name was *Aarav*. At first, he was just another face in the crowd, but something about the way he carried himself calm, mature, thoughtful drew me in. Over time, he became a comfort I didn't realize I was yearning for. I began to depend on him not just emotionally, but in a quiet, unspoken way where his opinions, his presence, even his silences began to fill the gaps I didn't know I had.

He became the person I would call for the smallest decisions. If something made me smile or hurt, he was the first one I would think of. Slowly, and perhaps inevitably, I began to fall for him. It was that silent kind of love not dramatic, not demanding, but deeply rooted. He wasn't just part of my life he became the lens through which I saw the world.

There's one evening I still remember like it happened yesterday.

I was sitting by the window of my tiny rented room after college, moonlight slipping through the curtain. The world was asleep, but my mind wasn't. I could feel the weight of unspoken things between us. We were still "together," but the emotional closeness we once had had started fading. And yet, I found myself smiling through the sadness, remembering how it all began how his gentle nature once made me feel buoyant, how the way he looked at me made me believe I mattered.

That night, I held back my tears, choosing instead to write down my feelings. I didn't call him. I didn't send a message. I simply poured it all onto the pages of my diary the heartbreak, the memories, the gratitude, the grief. And in that moment, something shifted in me. I was no longer just mourning a relationship I was growing through it.

As time passed, our differences grew louder. The things that once made us feel aligned began to clash. The emotional burden we carried his, mine became too much for either of us to bear. We tried to hold on. We tried to fix what we could. But *some stories are not meant to be rewritten only remembered for what they were.*

We both realized that love alone wasn't enough. Letting go was the kindest thing we could do for each other.

In that phase of silent separation, I found strength I didn't know I had. I walked through heartbreak like a storm, and came out on the other side with a quieter heart but a wiser soul.

But the pain didn't just stay in my heart it slowly affected my mind. The emotional load became too heavy to carry, and without realizing it, my mental health started to decline. I began to lose focus in my studies. I struggled to keep up, and in my third year of college, I failed one subject got a KT. It broke me at the time. I felt like I had let myself down.

But somehow and I truly believe this **God** was with me. I didn't give up. I retook the exam and passed. Not just the test, but the phase of life itself. It was one of the hardest chapters I lived through, but I emerged from it with a deeper understanding of myself and my inner strength.

Later, we shifted from Goa to Delhi. Initially, there was hope. A new place, a fresh start it felt like things might finally get better. But as days passed, reality struck harder than expected. The challenges only grew. Our relationship began to crack in ways that couldn't be mended. Family involvement, interference, emotional gaps everything started piling up. I tried — truly tried — to make it work, to hold on to what we once had. But nothing seemed to be enough.

What hurt the most was the constant interference from his past, who always had subtle ways of being present, even in our most private moments, it became painfully clear that my space was no longer mine.

I started feeling pity for myself not because of heartbreak, but because of how much of myself I was losing just to make things right. That's when it hit me: no matter how much you give, or how good your intentions are, some things are just not meant to last.

It's not about blaming anyone not even him. Sometimes, life simply unfolds according to destiny. No matter how much you try to resist it, what's meant to break will break and what's meant to stay, will stay with ease.

That day, I didn't just let go of a relationship I let go of an illusion.

That day, I didn't just let go of a relationship I let go of an illusion.

And in doing so, I found myself slowly, quietly, piece by

piece.

Pain doesn't always arrive with warning signs, and healing never asks for permission. But somewhere between holding on and letting go, I began to rediscover my own worth not as someone's partner, but as a woman who had survived, who had felt deeply, and who was still willing to love... herself.

I now understand:

Some chapters aren't meant to complete your story they're just meant to shape your soul.

Part of the destiny - The Shadow I Never Lost

The Shadow I Never Lost

Some friendships aren't chosen they arrive like shadows and never leave.

Just after school, and before the next chapters of adulthood unfolded, there was one friend who quietly anchored my life.

His name is Kuldeep.

He wasn't dramatic. He wasn't overly expressive. In fact, we fought a lot. Mostly because of me. I would throw my tantrums, say too much, feel too much... and he would just *listen*. Bear it. Hold it. Be there.

He became my constant my shadow.

When I started my career, unsure of my steps and often clouded by self-doubt, Kuldeep was the one who guided me. He helped me understand how to navigate early job roles, gave honest advice, and more than anything, reminded me that I was capable. In boardrooms and emotional breakdowns alike he was always a call away.

He never made a big deal of what he did but he did a lot. Quietly, steadily, consistently.

And in my personal life, too, he stood beside me like a protective wall. Whether it was heartbreak or hope, loss or joy, he was always there — not to fix it all, but just to be with me in it.

Life kept changing cities, jobs, relationships, heartbreaks, hopes. People came and went. But Kuldeep remained. Always there.

We're still together, as friends. Still fighting, still laughing, still calling each other names and making peace. He spends money with tight hands that much hasn't changed. But he's also one of the most caring and genuinely good humans I've had the luck to walk beside.

Even today, in the middle of a busy day or a silent night, when something good or bad happens, he's still the one I share it with. He listens the same way calmly, without judgment, and with heart.

I don't know how to explain this bond — because there are no ceremonies for friendship, no anniversaries to mark. But if you ask me who has stood beside me in silence, in chaos, in the days I didn't speak and in the nights I couldn't stop talking it's Kuldeep.

A real friend. A forever one.

How could I not add him in this book a book that holds my heart...!

CHAPTER FOUR

The Kindness of Strangers

After everything that happened in Delhi the emotional turmoil, the crumbling of a love I once thought would last I wasn't looking for anything new. Not love. Not friendship. Just silence.

I poured myself into my work at an IT company, keeping my head down and heart guarded. I became good at masking pain with professionalism, hiding my broken pieces beneath routines, meetings, and screen time. No one really noticed what I was going through but one person did.

Her name was *Meera*. She was my colleague, but more than that, she became a true friend. A kind of friend I didn't know still existed in a world that had tired me out. Meera had this quiet way of observing, of understanding me without needing explanations. She saw through the smile I wore to office every day. She noticed the silence behind my "I'm okay." And she never forced me to open up. She simply *stood by*.

There's something incredibly powerful about being *seen* when you think you're invisible.

She would often bring me little things a cup of chai, a sticky note with a motivational quote, or a chocolate when she thought I was low. And I started looking forward to those small moments of warmth, like they were pieces of sunshine in a room I had forgotten how to light.

One fine day, she came to me with a smile that held something more than just office gossip.

"I want to introduce you to someone," she said gently. "He's a simple guy... from another world altogether. I don't know why, but I feel like he might bring a smile to your life. Just as a friend."

I was hesitant, of course. I wasn't ready to let anyone in. But there was something about the way Meera said it not with pressure, but with care. A sense of protection. She wasn't pushing me toward someone she was pulling me back *toward myself*.

And so, I met him.

Let's call him *Dev*. A quiet soul, very grounded, unlike anyone I had ever known. There was a calmness in him that I had long forgotten. He wasn't loud with words or gestures, but he carried a sincerity that spoke louder than anything else. His simplicity was disarming. No pretenses. No games. Just honesty.

We began with small conversations casual talks during breaks, a few shared lunches, occasional walks after work. I didn't even realize when the walls I had so tightly built began to soften. He never asked me to share my past. But when I did, he simply listened without judgment, without pity.

That's what made the difference.

For the first time in a long time, I felt safe.

Not excited. Not swept off my feet. But safe.

And sometimes, that's the most romantic thing of all to be in someone's presence and feel at peace with who you are, scars and all.

With *Dev*, everything was different. There was no rush, no drama, no overwhelming promises. It was all... gentle.

He didn't ask for anything from me not my stories, not explanations, not even time. He simply showed up. Consistently. Softly. Every day, in small ways that made big changes in how I began to see myself again.

There's one moment I remember vividly.

It had been a rough day. A small trigger at work had brought back the wave of past grief. I was quiet, withdrawn something Dev must have noticed, even though I tried to hide it. After work, instead of saying anything, he walked beside me and handed me a folded note. He said only one thing:

"You don't need to talk. Just read this when you're ready."

It wasn't a love letter or anything dramatic. Just a few words, scribbled with genuine care:

"You don't have to prove your worth to anyone.
You've already survived more than most people can imagine.
If today hurts, let it. I'll be around when tomorrow feels lighter."

I don't remember how long I stood there holding that paper, but something broke inside me in the best way. The kind of breaking that frees you.

With him, I didn't feel judged. I didn't feel "damaged." I simply felt human.

Our friendship blossomed into something deeper over time though neither of us rushed to name it. It wasn't a fairy tale. It was *real*. And real, as I had learned by now, is messy and beautiful in equal measure.

Dev helped me re-learn trust. And not just in others — in myself.

Through this period, Meera remained my silent pillar, always watching from the sidelines with her warm smile and knowing eyes. To this day, I believe she was sent into my life as a quiet guardian — someone who didn't rescue me, but reminded me that I *could* rescue myself.

Sometimes, it's not the person you fall in love with who changes your life.
It's the one who holds the mirror up and says, "You deserve better. You always did."

Dev was unlike anyone I had ever met.

When I poured my past into words every heartbreak, every broken piece, every scar I still carried he didn't flinch. He didn't interrupt. He didn't try to fix me.

He just listened.

And in that silence, I found more healing than I had in years of noise.

He never told me what to do. He never offered advice unless I asked. He never questioned the "whys" of my life or the choices I had made. He simply gave me space, space to be who I was, without shame, without apology. That's all I ever needed, and all I never knew I was allowed to ask for.

I told him everything the lingering shadows of my past relationship, the nights I cried myself to sleep, the guilt I carried, the emotional bruises I had stopped showing to the world. And still, he stayed. Not out of pity, but presence.

He saw me not for my pain, but for my potential.

"You have wings," he once said softly, "I know you want to fly. And I'll be the wind if you let me not the cage."

That one sentence shattered me... and stitched me back together.

His simplicity was his strength. While I was tangled in emotions I couldn't always explain, he held a quiet faith in me a faith that helped me start believing in myself again.

There were no grand gestures between us, no scripted confessions. Yet, in the pauses of our conversations, we said more than words ever could.

We shared silences. We completed thoughts without finishing sentences.
We existed not to fix each other but to remind one another that healing was possible.

There was no certainty about where this path would take us no labels, no pressure. Just one day at a time. Just one moment of trust layered over another.

And slowly, I began to feel something I had not felt in years:
Hope.

"Some people don't enter your life to stay.
They arrive to awaken the part of you that forgot how to dream."

With *Dev*, I remembered my worth.
I remembered that love isn't loud.
It's steady.
It's kind.
It's the hand that doesn't hold you back but lifts you toward the sky

(Turning Point: When Friendship Became Love)

Days turned into months, and without us realizing it, the bond between me and Dev grew roots — steady, silent, and strong. There was no announcement, no sudden "I love you," no dramatic moment that changed everything. It was subtler than that. Like the way dawn breaks without noise... just light, spreading quietly across the sky.

One evening, we were walking after work something we had started doing more often. The city was busy, as usual, but around us, there was a strange stillness. We weren't talking, just listening to each other's silences, letting them fill the space where words once tried too hard. And then, he paused and looked at me really looked.

"I don't want to walk beside you only for today," he said. "I want to walk with you... through it all."

That was the moment.

The moment where something shifted in the air between us soft but certain.

My heart didn't race; it slowed down.
Like it finally found a rhythm it could rest in.

It wasn't a proposal. It wasn't poetry. It was presence and a promise. The kind of promise that doesn't need a ceremony to be sacred.

From that day onward, we weren't just two people healing side by side. We became *one direction*. One path. One journey.

His calm became my calm. My dreams became his priority. His gentleness wrapped around my old wounds like quiet prayer. And every time I doubted myself every time the ghosts of my past relationships whispered in my ear he would remind me, not with words, but with actions, that I was *not broken*, just beautifully rebuilt.

Even my fears began to soften.

I no longer feared love.
Because this love didn't demand.
It gave.

It didn't expect me to change.
It allowed me to grow.

I realized then: Love isn't always fire and lightning. Sometimes, love is water the thing that nourishes you slowly, patiently, until you begin to bloom.

"Sometimes the person you least expect becomes the one you trust the most.
Not because they change your life, but because they help

you remember who you were before the world told you to forget."

With Dev, I began writing a new chapter — not in a book, but in myself.

And for the first time in years, I didn't feel like a character in someone else's story.

I was finally living *my own.*

CHAPTER FIVE

Becoming Her — The Woman I Was Meant to Be

(Love, Faith, and the Courage to Begin Again)

Building a life with Dev wasn't some grand plan it was a leap of faith built on scattered pieces of two broken pasts. After many long discussions and endless tiny disagreements, we finally reached a place of quiet understanding. I was the hesitant one the one who feared trusting life again. I kept wondering: *"Can I really start over? Do I deserve this happiness?"*

Dev never tried to convince me with words.
He didn't promise me the stars or build dreamy castles in the air.
He just stayed.

In every silence, every setback, and every tear-filled night, his unspoken promise stood strong:

"I'm here. No matter what."

There were no costly gifts, no grand declarations. What he gave me was rarer — his presence, unwavering and true. And at that stage in life, it was all I needed.

We didn't have money.

We didn't have a house.

In truth, we didn't even have a plan.

But what we did have was a shared belief that somehow, together, we would find the way.

Dev started working at a small coffee shop. The income wasn't much, just enough for basic needs. We found a tiny room to rent small, but filled with warmth and laughter. That room became our world. We cooked simple meals, shared stories under a single dim light, and built dreams brick by emotional brick.

In that space, there was no pretense. Just two souls creating a life in their own way, in their own rhythm.

People came and went.

Some doubted us.

Some judged us.

Some mocked our situation our lack of money, our living condition, our unorthodox beginning.

But none of that could touch us. We had something more powerful than approval we had faith. In each other. In love. In *us*.

"When love is honest and hearts are clean, even the winds bow in respect."

Slowly, without any rush, life began unfolding.

Each passing day felt like a step sometimes small, sometimes tiring, but always forward. Our financial situation improved, piece by piece. We began understanding not just each other's joys, but also our deepest scars. And eventually, we got married not because the world needed a label on our love, but because *we wanted to celebrate it with the world.*

Years passed.

And yet, even now, when I look back at those early days

those nights in the tiny rented room, sharing hopes over chai, encouraging each other after exhausting days I realize...

That was when we were richest.

We didn't just build a life.
We built home one filled with patience, respect, and unconditional love.

We never needed grand parties to celebrate.
For us, happiness was in the smallest things.

Every month, when Dev received his modest salary and the little perks from his coffee shop job, it felt like a festival. We would look forward to that one evening not for the money, but for the ritual of joy it brought.

We'd step out with childlike excitement to buy food not luxury, just one full meal where we didn't have to worry about budgeting each bite. Sitting cross-legged on the floor of our little room, unwrapping the parcel of food, we'd laugh, talk, and feast like kings.

It was never about what was on the plate it was about what was between us: love, effort, and togetherness.

Sometimes, we'd recall those moments days later a smile would cross our faces, and our eyes would meet in silent recognition of a memory too deep to explain. These were thegolden parts of our story the kind of memories that stay etched in your soul, unspoken yet unforgettable.

"Not all rich lives are wrapped in silk. Some are stitched together with shared struggle and quiet joys and those are the ones that last."

These memories of waiting, sharing, and simply being are not just moments.
They are our roots, anchoring us in humility and love, no matter how far we go in life.

As days passed, change came slowly and then all at once.

I received a job offer, one that paid even more than what Dev was earning at that time. He was genuinely thrilled for me, no traces of ego, no insecurity just pride in his eyes and his usual quiet smile. I still remember how he said,

"We'll move into a better place with your first salary."

And we did.

With that first paycheck, we found a slightly bigger house modest, but with space to breathe and dream. It was our next step, and this time, we were building not just a shelter, but a life together.

Dev's younger sister a sweet, simple girl came to help us move. She didn't know all our struggles, our emotional baggage, or the depth of what we had overcome. But her presence, her small efforts to assist us, felt like love. As Dev's sister, she became a part of my growing circle of care. That day wasn't just a shift of house it was a step up the staircase of our life.

Then came a day that shook us quietly I found out I was expecting.

We stared at each other, blank, not with excitement, but with questions. Were we ready? Could we really raise a child in this unstable phase of our lives? Our hearts said one thing, but reality whispered something else.

Dev, unsure like me, called his father. Hoping for a guiding voice, for reassurance, for a direction.

His father was honest, but not comforting.

"You're still struggling... how will you manage a baby? You're just starting your life."

No judgment. Just realism. But somewhere in my heart, a small thread of hope had quietly tied itself to the thought *What if he had said yes? What if he had said, "Don't worry, I'm here for you both"?*

Maybe our path would have been different. Maybe we would have raised that child.

But we didn't know better. We were young. Confused. Caught in fear.

I took the pills.

It happened quietly, like many things in a woman's life do. Without drama. Without ceremony. Just pain the silent kind.

We didn't cry much that day. But something inside us changed.

Maybe it was maturity. Maybe it was grief disguised as strength.

But we knew this was a moment we'd carry quietly in our hearts forever.

"Some decisions aren't right or wrong they're just what you can handle with the version of yourself that exists at that time."

Even today, we don't blame each other or anyone else. We just... understand.

That day taught us what books and elders don't. It taught us that life doesn't wait for you to be ready it just *comes*, and you either step forward with it, or let it pass and find peace in the decision you made.

CHAPTER SIX

A New Beginning

One fine night, we were sitting close, sharing funny horror stories laughing so hard it echoed in the quiet room. The kind of laughter that makes your chest ache and your eyes water. As the night turned into early morning, tiredness wrapped around us like a soft blanket, and we fell asleep side by side.

When the morning light peeked through the window, I saw a board pasted on the outside wall. My heart stopped as I read the words: *"Vacate this apartment immediately. Reconstruction planned."*

A heavy silence fell between us. Fear and uncertainty hovered, but there was something else too an unspoken bond that held us together.

He looked at me with wide eyes. "What... what if we have nowhere to go?"

I reached for his hand, feeling its warmth steady my own trembling. "Hey, look at me. We're together, right? That's what matters. We'll find a way. We always do."

He squeezed my hand tightly, a small smile breaking through his worry. "I believe that. It's like the universe is testing us... but it's also guiding us."

That day, he skipped work and went straight to a rental agency. Hours later, he came back, eyes shining with hope.

"I found a place," he said. "The agent said they have a house for rent."

I swallowed the knot in my throat. The deposit money wasn't enough. But hearing the hope in his voice made my heart swell.

"We don't have enough for the deposit," I said softly. "What if they say no?"

"We'll ask," he said confidently. "We can't lose hope now."

Together, we walked into the agency. The girl behind the desk looked at us kindly as we explained.

"We can pay the deposit in two parts," he said. "Please help us talk to the owner."

She smiled warmly. "I'll arrange a meeting. Just be honest and sincere."

Two days later, we met the owner. My heart pounded as I handed him my visiting card.

"I work in IT," I said steadily, "and we both have stable jobs. We promise to pay the deposit in two parts."

He studied us for a moment, then nodded. "Alright. You can move in."

Relief and joy flooded me so deeply I felt like I might cry. I looked at him and said,
"We did it. We really did it."

He pulled me close, and I rested my head on his shoulder. "Feels like the universe is smiling on us right now."

I smiled, feeling a quiet warmth spread inside me, like a gentle light that comes when you know you're exactly where you're meant to be.
"Maybe this is what destiny looks like. We're exactly where we're supposed to be... together."

He looked out at the empty house, keys in his hand. "Empty now, but we'll fill it—with memories, with laughter, with everything we dream of."

And standing there, hearts full and hands entwined, we felt the presence of something greater a silent promise from the universe that as long as we have each other, everything will be okay. We stood in the empty room, the faint echo of our footsteps bouncing off bare walls. The keys felt heavy in his palm not just metal, but a symbol of hope, trust, and a new beginning.

I leaned against the wall, closing my eyes for a moment. The silence was soft, almost sacred. Outside, the world kept moving, but in here, time seemed to slow.

He sat beside me on the cold floor, pulling me close. Our breaths mingled in the stillness.

"Do you feel it?" I whispered. "Like the universe has been quietly working behind the scenes, pulling strings we couldn't see."

He nodded slowly. "It's like every small struggle, every sleepless night, every doubt... it all led us here. Not by chance, but by design."

I reached for his hand, tracing invisible patterns on his skin. "I think this is what faith feels like not just believing in a higher power, but knowing deep inside that we're never truly alone."

A soft smile touched his lips. "Together, we're stronger than any challenge. And even when it feels like the world is shifting beneath our feet, we have each other and that's enough."

We sat quietly, wrapped in a shared stillness that needed no words. The empty house wasn't just a place it was a canvas for our dreams, a shelter for our hopes.

And in that moment, beneath the calm and the promise of what's to come, we felt the gentle presence of something greater, guiding us gently forward one step, one breath, one day at a time.

We stood side by side, watching the world wake up.

In that quiet moment, our hearts beat with the same hopeful rhythm a promise to build a life here, not just of walls and roofs, but of love, trust, and faith.

No matter what comes next, we knew we were ready. Together, and always moving forward.

Destiny's Quiet Dance

In the stillness of our night,
Whispers linger, soft and light
Memories of battles fought,
Dreams we held, the hope they brought.

Hands entwined, a gentle grace,
Finding warmth in shared embrace,
Not alone, though shadows fall,
The universe has heard our call.

Winding paths, not straight or clear,
Every step both joy and fear,
Yet through trials, through silent pleas,
We've found our way with steady ease.

This is destiny, I say,
Not a line, but shades of grey
Miracles in every turn,
Lessons waiting to be learned.

So here we stand at dawn's first light,
Hearts aligned, souls burning bright,
Together strong, come what may
Building love day by day.

CHAPTER SEVEN

A New Shelter, A New Test

The joy of unlocking the door to our new home was like unwrapping a gift we never imagined we'd receive. It had no furniture, no comforts but it had four walls, a roof, and the echo of our laughter bouncing off empty rooms. That was enough. It was a fresh canvas. And in those first few weeks, we painted it with hope.

Dev and I were growing more than just as a couple—we were becoming a team, a quiet force of resilience. Evenings were spent lying on a mattress on the floor, talking about dreams, futures, the way the stars blinked through the window like they were watching over us.

"Do you think God is smiling at us right now?" I whispered once.

He turned, hand in mine. "I think He's walking with us."

But life doesn't walk in a straight line for long.

One morning, the phone rang. It was my elder brother. His voice was unsteady, edged with panic.

"Maa is in the hospital... It's serious."

The world around me blurred. Dev was already standing beside me, no words needed.

Within hours, we were on a train to Gujarat—with no reservations, no sleep, no time to think, just a determination that felt heavier than any suitcase we carried.

When we reached the hospital, I saw her.

My mother.

Lying unconscious in the MICU, saline lines piercing her skin, surrounded by the beeping of machines and the cold air of uncertainty. My heart broke into pieces I didn't know how to gather.

We had little money, barely enough for ourselves, but we managed—somehow. We ran around for medicines, paid bills, found corners to sit and rest, found strength in each other.

For ten days, we lived in a blur of prayers and pain.

And when Maa finally opened her eyes and whispered our names, I felt like the universe exhaled with relief. We discharged her and brought her to my brother's house, hoping she could recover there.

But soon, his discomfort showed. "I don't think I can take care of her like you can," he said.

It hurt.

This was the same woman who had weathered storms for us, stood unshaken in the face of every struggle, and now—her own son hesitated.

Still, I understood. Not everyone has the same capacity. Not everyone is built to hold what others cannot.

I told him, "Once she can walk, I'll take her with me. She's my responsibility too."

That night, Dev held me as I cried. Not because I was angry. But because love—real love—asks us to carry burdens that aren't always ours, simply because we can.

And that's what life was now asking of us.

CHAPTER EIGHT

A Full House, A Fuller Heart

Weeks passed, and Maa slowly regained her strength. The day she took her first few steps without help, I felt a silent celebration within me. Not loud, not showy—but sacred.

True to my word, we brought her home.

Our little rented space, once echoing only with our laughter and dreams, now carried the scent of warm turmeric milk, the gentle hum of old bhajans, and the fragile rhythm of an old woman's breath as she slept peacefully beside us.

There was no guest room, no extra bed—just corners we rearranged, routines we reshaped, and hearts we opened even wider.

I still remember the moment she stepped in.

She looked around, eyes a little uncertain but grateful. Dev stepped forward, placing her bag down gently and saying, "This is your home now too, Maa."

She looked at him, then at me, and for a long moment said nothing.

Then she smiled small, tired, but filled with something I hadn't seen in her in a long time: safety.

Some nights, I would watch her sleep, her breath shallow but calm, and I would whisper quiet thanks to the universe.

"This is what we were meant to do," I said once to Dev.

He nodded, pulling me close. "This... this is love. Not just between us, but through us."

Of course, it wasn't easy. There were medicines, doctor visits, sudden fevers, and days when exhaustion crept into my bones. But there was also peace—because Maa was with us. Because even when life stripped us of convenience, it never stripped us of purpose.

We shared our meals, our time, and our stories with her. Dev, who once worried about how to care for someone so fragile, now brought her tea, wrapped her shawl around her shoulders, and learned to listen to her tales from the past.

And Maa... she bloomed, slowly. Not fully but enough. Enough to fill the space with her presence.

Our small home had transformed. Not with furniture or wealth, but with something far richer.

It became a sanctuary of love, sacrifice, and the kind of togetherness only trials can teach.

CHAPTER NINE

The Quiet Rise

Life in the new house began with a warm glow. Though it had no furniture, the emptiness was filled with joy and quiet dreams. We would often sit on the floor, Dev and I, sipping tea from borrowed cups, planning what this blank canvas of a home could one day become.

But destiny, as always, had a different path charted for us.

One afternoon, my phone rang it was my elder brother. His voice was tense.

"Mom's been hospitalized... it's serious."

Everything blurred. I dropped everything and looked at Dev.

Without hesitation, he said, "We're going. Now."

With barely any money in hand and no train reservations, we boarded the next available train to Gujarat. I remember how we sat on the floor near the train door all night, holding onto each other and hope.

When we reached the hospital, seeing my mother in the MICU shook something deep within me. Tubes, saline bottles, machines all trying to breathe life into the woman who had once been the very breath of our childhood. She lay unconscious, unaware that her daughter had come rushing back, heart trembling, hands empty yet willing to give everything.

Despite not having enough finances, we did what we could. Medicine bills, travel, temporary shelter—we arranged it all, bit by bit. And through it all, Dev was by my side, tireless and silent in his support. Those ten days changed something in me. Watching my mother fight for life reminded me of her strength... and taught me my own.

Eventually, she stabilized, and we took her to my brother's house. I had expected relief, a shared sense of responsibility. But instead, I was told, "You should take Maa. I don't think I can care for her like you can."
It was painful this quiet shifting of duty. But I knew... she was mine.
"Let her walk again," I said gently. "Once she can stand on her own, I'll bring her with me."

That day, as we walked back to our rented room, I looked up at the sky and whispered,
"I know You're watching. Just stay with us a little longer."

CHAPTER TEN

A New Dawn

Bringing Maa home marked a new beginning one filled with tenderness, adjustments, and silent sacrifices. It wasn't easy. With her medical needs, the cost of living, and our small income, everything felt tight—money, time, even energy. But not love. That, somehow, kept growing.

We lived carefully, managing every rupee with care. But slowly, life responded.

One fine day, a call came. A job opportunity unexpected and promising. I got it. A better salary, better hours. When I told Dev, he just smiled and said, "Told you... good things are coming."

That month, we bought our first piece of secondhand furniture—a little wooden cupboard. Then a table. A fan. One small item at a time, we started shaping the house into a home. Nothing fancy. But each object held pride, effort, and belief.

We'd often sit with Maa, watching TV on a secondhand set, laughing together.

No luxury. Just life. Full, raw, and real.

CHAPTER ELEVEN

The Heart Learns New Rhythms

The days began to stretch differently after Ma moved in. Our home, once echoing with just the two of us our laughter, our silences, our shared chaos now pulsed with a new rhythm. It was softer in parts, more patient, and filled with quiet care.

Morning tea was no longer rushed. I would often sit beside Ma, holding her hand, helping her adjust her shawl, watching her eyes trace the slow dance of light on the floor. Dev, always intuitive, found ways to keep her comfortable he made her laugh, teased her gently, and even tried to master her favorite recipes.

There were days of exhaustion, yes. Financial strains hadn't fully disappeared, and balancing work, home, and emotional fatigue wasn't easy. But amidst it all, something profound was growing an unspoken bond that wove us tighter together. We were no longer just a couple in love. We had become a family with responsibilities, with purpose, with a deeper sense of belonging.

Sometimes at night, I would sit by the window after everyone had gone to bed, the city lights flickering far away. I'd whisper silent thank-yous to the universe for

Dev's steady hands, for Ma's slow recovery, and for the strength I never knew lived inside me.

Love was changing shape. It wasn't just flowers and stolen kisses anymore it was warm meals, quiet reassurances, held hands, and shared responsibilities.

We were learning. Growing. Quietly, still, we rose.

At first, her footsteps were faint—fragile like her body, which was still healing. But slowly, they grew firmer. Her appetite improved. She smiled more often. And in those moments over a cup of tea, a soft laugh, or a shared plate of fruit I saw something sacred return to her eyes: peace.

She often said, *"Here, I feel like I've come home again."* That one line gave me the strength to juggle everything—office work, home chores, medicine routines, and long nights. Her joy became my courage.

Dev was my silent strength through it all. He never made it feel like a burden. He would come back from work and sit by her side, listening to her stories with genuine warmth. I often watched them from the kitchen door him laughing, her eyes lighting up and I'd smile quietly, grateful for this unexpected bond between them.

Yes, finances were still tight. Yes, we still made choices between needs and dreams. But we had found something rare togetherness that could heal.

In this little home with secondhand furniture and first-rate love, we were building something sacred. Not perfect. But real.

We were healing, too. As she rose, so did we. Quietly, still we rose.

The Light Within Our Walls

Day by day, my mother's health began to improve. Her diet got better, and so did her spirit. There was something deeply comforting about having her with us her presence filled our home with warmth that no furniture or decoration ever could. Even though she was living with Parkinson's, she never let it define her. She insisted on helping with the household chores in whatever way she could, always aware that both Dev and I returned home exhausted from long workdays.

"Let me do this much," she would say softly, her voice trembling but full of determination. "You both do enough."

She often spoke of the pain and struggles she had endured in her earlier days times when care was scarce, and emotional support was even scarcer. As she recounted those stories, I could see the sorrow in her eyes, but there was no bitterness in her heart.

"It's okay," she'd say, placing her fragile hand on mine. "No matter what happened then, all I want now is for you to be happy. I want to see you flourish. I know you will."

Her blessings became the quiet power behind my strength. I believed that her words carried grace, and that they shaped the good that slowly began to bloom in our lives. Every evening, as I prayed, I asked for one thing: that God grant her a long life maybe even a hundred years so that she could experience the joy she had been denied in the past. I wanted her to see the sunrises of peace, to sit in the passenger seat on long car rides, smiling as the wind touched her face. I wanted her to feel what it meant to be cherished, not just as a mother, but as a person who had given so much without ever asking for anything in return.

We were building a life not just for ourselves, but for her too. And in those moments of quiet understanding between us, I knew that God was still writing something beautiful.

Sometimes, healing doesn't come in grand gestures it arrives in small acts of love:
a glass of water placed without asking,

a story repeated for comfort,
a blessing whispered into the air.
    In my mother's quiet efforts, I found resilience.
In her presence, I discovered what it means to be home.
    She, who once carried me through storms,
now rests in the calm we built together.
And I still her child carry her dreams like folded prayers in
my pocket,
waiting to unfold them, one by one, into the light.

CHAPTER TWELVE

The Weight of Hope

One evening at home, shortly after Dev has returned from meeting the man who promised him a job abroad.]

Dev (quietly):

"Aarti... I met someone today. Near the office. He said I can get a job in the shipping industry. Abroad. He knows people. But... I'll have to do a diploma first."

Aarti (looking up, cautious):

"A diploma? What kind of job is it? Is it real?"

Dev (nodding):

"He says it's in rigs or ships big money. But I need to pay for training, licenses, passport formalities. It starts with 10,000. Then more as we go."

Aarti (pauses, thinking):

"We just started to breathe easier... we've only begun buying our second-hand furniture. Do you really believe this is worth the risk?"

Dev (sincerely):

"I don't want us to live like this forever. If this works out... we can finally build something bigger. I want to give you that life."

Aarti (after a long silence):

"Then we'll do it. But we'll be careful. No matter how long it takes just promise me we won't lose ourselves chasing something that isn't real."

We walked forward that day hand in hand not into certainty, but into a gamble fueled by hope. Every payment we made, every document we arranged, felt like a small brick in the wall of a dream. We told ourselves it would be temporary. A few months, maybe a year. A little suffering for long-term peace.

But one demand led to another. First the diploma, then certifications, then expensive licenses. Every time we sent money, we waited for the return. It never came.

For nearly seven years, we lived in repayment. Loan after loan. Hope after disappointment. Dev blamed himself, silently, every night. I saw it in his eyes. And yet, I never blamed him. Because I knew we did it together. We believed. Together.

There were nights we couldn't sleep, not from fear, but exhaustion. Mental, emotional, financial. The world outside never saw the weight we carried inside. But still, each morning, we rose. Quietly. Again.

ust when we thought we had weathered the hardest parts, life placed another storm at our doorstep.

I still remember that day sharp pain twisting in my side, my breath shallow, the hospital lights blinding. What I thought might be a new beginning turned into a cruel pause. The doctors spoke in hushed tones. "Ectopic pregnancy," they said. Emergency surgery. One fallopian tube removed. And with it, a part of me I had long protected hope.

The silence on the hospital bed was unbearable. My hand instinctively reached for Dev's. He was there, quietly holding my fingers, not speaking, not blinking his grip tighter than usual, as if to hold together everything that was breaking inside me.

Aarti (quietly, eyes closed):
"Why us again? Why does every time we rise, something pulls us back down?"

Dev (softly, his voice cracking):
"Because we're strong enough to rise again."

I didn't reply. I couldn't. The physical pain was one thing but the ache in my heart, the mourning of a child I never got to hold, and the mourning of the *chance* to dream again that ran deeper.

The doctor's words kept echoing in my ears:
"Chances are low now. With one tube, it will be difficult to conceive naturally."

My heart rebelled. I wanted to scream, to hit something, to question the god I had always trusted. Why? Why now? Why this? Why when we were already crawling through borrowed finances, lost promises, and mounting loans?

I withdrew into myself for weeks. I became short-tempered, frustrated. Dev was always gentle but I pushed him away with my moods. Not out of anger at him but at the weight of my own helplessness. At how unfair life seemed.

Aarti (one evening, breaking down):
"I had so many dreams... just a small home, a child, a normal life. Was that too much to ask?"

Dev (pulling her close):
"No dream is too much, Arti. Maybe it's delayed. Not denied. We'll still find a way."

Those seven years felt like a slow drowning. Every time we thought we'd reached the shore, the waves pulled us under again. Yet, through the darkness, one truth stood tall Dev never let go of my hand.

And somewhere in that pain, in the frustration, in the long nights where I wept quietly on the pillow beside him, I found a strange kind of strength. Not the loud, screaming kind but a quiet, determined one.

We may not have had much money. We may not have had answers. But we had *us*. And perhaps that was the one thing the world could never take.

CHAPTER THIRTEEN

Silent Storms, Unspoken Strength

"You think he'll call today?" I asked, not really expecting an answer as I stared blankly at the fan spinning above.

Dev shook his head. "It's been a week. He said next week for the papers. Maybe tomorrow." But I could see it in his eyes the same fear I had in mine. We were both hanging onto hope like it was the last branch on a cliff.

Every month brought a new expense. A new request. A new form. A new promise. And we paid from loans, from borrowed hands, from the little savings we stitched together from our paychecks. Lakh after lakh, thinking this was an investment for our future. A way out. A chance to breathe.

But instead of open air, we found ourselves suffocating.

During those years, something inside me began to change. Or maybe break.

And then came the day the doctor sat me down, eyes soft but words sharp. "It was an ectopic pregnancy. We had to operate immediately. One fallopian tube has been removed."

The words pierced deeper than the scalpel.

Later that night, I lay curled on the hospital bed, staring at the IV drip, whispering to no one, *"Why? Haven't we already lost enough?"*

Dev held my hand. He didn't say anything. He didn't need to. His silence was stronger than any spoken word. But inside, I was crumbling.

"I didn't ask for luxury, God. I asked for peace. A child. A small home. A moment of joy that didn't vanish in bills and interest rates."

Days turned into months. Months into years. And we kept going. Like tired wheels that refused to stop spinning. I found myself arguing more not with him, but at him. My frustration, my helplessness, my broken dreams they all needed a place to land. And he stood there, quiet, absorbing it all.

And yet... we never stopped holding each other through the tears.

That's what saved us. That's what kept the flame from going out completely.

Even in our darkest hour, we remained a team wounded, yes, but together.

There were nights I would sit alone by the window, listening to the city hum in the distance the kind of hum that didn't care if someone's world had fallen apart. I remember placing my palm on my stomach, not out of hope, but in memory of what could've been.

Dev would bring me tea quietly and sit beside me without asking questions. We didn't speak much those days not because we had nothing to say, but because our silence held more truth than words ever could.

But life, in its quiet wisdom, doesn't always rush to heal. It mends slowly, gently like sunlight creeping in after a storm.

One evening, as I returned home from work, tired and lost in thoughts, I saw a small plant pot near our door. A bright little marigold had bloomed in it. I stood staring at it. I didn't remember planting it. Dev came up behind me and said, "I just thought... maybe we need something that grows."

That night, I cried. Not from pain. But because something shifted. A soft breeze of peace touched my chest for the first time in years. Maybe we weren't where we wanted to be, but we hadn't given up. And that meant something.

Slowly, Dev began to take up small freelance assignments odd IT work here and there, and sometimes people even reached out to him for help with computer systems or software issues. Nothing steady, but it was something. And I, too, received an opportunity to handle a small project in my office independently. That recognition, however minor, felt like a door cracking open.

We didn't leap forward we inched.

But every inch was earned. Every smile was fought for.

And as the weight began to shift, our hands found each other again not just to survive, but to walk forward with a little less burden, and a little more hope.

CHAPTER FOURTEEN

The Sound of Life

In the middle of everything the wreckage of past dreams, the slow rebuilding of hope, the loans, the silences life whispered again.

I had missed a few days. My body felt... different. I didn't want to think much of it, but Dev noticed.

"You think it could be...?" he asked softly one night.

I didn't answer. I couldn't. The last time, hope had betrayed me. It had left me on a hospital bed, clutching at nothing, bleeding from more than just my body.

Still, a quiet instinct nudged us toward the truth. And then, that morning came the morning that would forever change the way we looked at time.

The clinic opened at 10, our sonography appointment was for 11, but we were there by 9:30 hearts racing faster than the ticking clock. We sat side by side on the hospital bench, our hands tightly clasped, our palms damp with anxious prayers.

I whispered inside my mind, *"Please, not again. Please give me one more chance, just one."*

The sonographer called my name. My knees trembled as I lay down. Dev stood beside me, his fingers gripping the edge of the bed, pretending to be calm.

The screen lit up. Cold gel on my skin. A probe. A pause.

Then the most beautiful sound filled the room — rhythmic, certain, full of life.

"See? Hear that? That's your baby's heartbeat," the sonographer said with a smile.

I gasped. Dev froze. We looked at each other, speechless.

Tears welled up, but they didn't fall. They sat right at the edge like we did for so many years holding on.

We stepped out of the room into the quiet corridor. Dev looked at me with eyes wide and soft. He didn't speak grand things. He just said, "Now you have to take care. Everything is good."

I nodded. Not because I knew what to say, but because that was all my heart could manage.

That day, the world didn't change outside the city still rushed, the bills still waited but inside us, something sacred had begun.

A heartbeat.

A promise.

A miracle born in the quiet after the storm.

CHAPTER FIFTEEN

Hope in One Hand, Burden in the Other

Pregnancy, they say, is a beautiful journey and it is.

But no one prepares you for the weight of carrying a child while also carrying the crushing burden of debt, disappointment, and uncertain futures.

Every day brought something new: a check-up, another strip of pills, iron and calcium supplements, scans, reports, travel, consultations. The doctor's clinic became my second home. The bills, our constant visitors.

While my body was nurturing life, our life outside felt like it was quietly crumbling.

The cost of survival rose with each heartbeat I carried inside me. Yet that same heartbeat gave me the strength to keep walking for myself, for Dev, for the life growing within.

"Let's do something," Dev said one evening, as we stared at a growing stack of unpaid bills.

"With what?" I asked gently.

"Whatever we have. Let's start something small... a business, maybe. Anything that can grow."

We took the risk. Scraped together what little we had. Joined hands in partnership with someone Dev trusted. We dreamed again, just a little enough to breathe.

For a moment, it felt like maybe, just maybe, the tide would turn.

But it didn't.

The business failed. Another loss. Another silence between us at dinner. Another round of explanations to people we had borrowed from.

And Roshan the same man who promised Dev a job on the rig continued his empty reassurances like a broken record.

"Next week, Dev... I just spoke to the guy."

"Few more days, papers are under process."

"Just wait it's happening."

Days turned to months. Months into years. Still nothing.

But we didn't let go of hope. We couldn't afford to. Hope was the only thing we didn't have to buy.

I remember lying on the bed, hand on my stomach, whispering to the little life inside me.

"You chose us, little one. You didn't come by mistake. So we will rise. One day, you'll know how much we fought to bring you into this world."

Dev would sit beside me late at night, quiet, scrolling through job portals, looking for opportunities, anything, anywhere.

He whispers, "Just wait... one day, all this will be a story. A past."

And I believed him. Even when I didn't know how.

From Womb to World

Even with the weight of debt and dreams deferred, I held
on.

I held on to the life growing inside me.
To the hope that this child would bring a new beginning.
To the doctor the one who had once saved me from the
trauma of an ectopic pregnancy, now guiding me through
every step like a protective angel.

When the eighth month approached, she looked at me
with deep concern in her eyes.
"You will need a C-section," she said softly. "It's safer for
both of you. We won't risk complications."

I nodded. I had no fear left. Only surrender.

The day of delivery came like a quiet storm.
They wheeled me into the operation theatre. I felt the
chill of the steel table. The anesthesia numbed my body
but not my soul. I could still feel it. Not pain. But
presence.
The slicing, the shifting the wait.

And then... the cry.

A cry that was mine. That was his. That was ours.

My baby boy. Fair like morning light. Eyes wide, searching
the world he had just entered. He didn't cry too long he
was too curious, too alive.

Tears spilled from my eyes. Was this a dream? Or had God finally answered me, after all these years of asking?

Outside, Dev was told: "It's a boy."
He handed out sweets like he'd been carrying them in his pockets forever, waiting for this moment.

But I... I was still in that room a mother now, lying in stillness, replaying everything we had endured to reach here.

He was beside me soon. Soft, warm, tiny. His head rested against me like it always belonged there.

The journey had truly begun.

And yet, even in this sacred moment, a crack surfaced.

One evening, while I was talking to Dev about something small, his stepmother a woman who had never played a mother's role in his life chose that moment to interrupt, correct, involve herself. Her voice carried weight, but not warmth.

Inside me, something snapped.

I believe in reflecting back whatever is given to me be it love, respect, or distance.
And I had already decided: *You don't earn a place in someone's new life just by holding a title. You earn it through love, presence, and responsibility.*

I wasn't angry. Just clear.

This was our journey now mine, Dev's, and our son's.
A new family. Built from struggle. Rooted in truth.

We had fallen, broken, healed.
And now, we had risen quietly, powerfully again.

CHAPTER SIXTEEN

Tiny Hands, Giant Heartbeats

The hospital room was quiet except for the soft cooing of a newborn our son, our miracle, lay beside me, his tiny fingers curling instinctively around mine. After years of turbulence, this moment felt like a quiet pause in a storm.

I watched Dev as he stood near the window, holding a box of sweets, smiling but also lost in thought. The weight of the world still rested on our shoulders, but in that instant, we had something beautiful that was truly ours.

"Can you believe he's here?" I whispered, my voice fragile from the surgery.

Dev turned toward me, eyes glistening. "I still can't believe we're parents. He's perfect... just like you said he'd be."

Despite the warmth in his voice, I sensed a distance not coldness, but a kind of quiet fear. The months leading to this day had emptied our savings, piled on loans, and strained us in ways words couldn't explain. I had expected Dev to be my rock during the delivery, but he was caught between his hopes and the weight of everything that had gone wrong.

I tried to stay present in the moment, to soak in the scent of my baby's soft skin, to let his tiny breaths remind me that life could still be kind. But inside, I was aching from the stitches, from fatigue, from unspoken emotions, and from the silent expectations I had placed on both of us.

Back at home, our world rearranged itself. Days and nights blurred into feeding, changing, and rocking. The silence of responsibility was louder than ever.

One night, as I sat rocking my son to sleep, I looked up at Dev and asked gently, "Do you ever feel like we've aged ten years in just a few?"

He sighed, sitting beside me. "Yes... but then I see him smile, and I feel like maybe everything's worth it."

We didn't have luxury. We didn't even have peace all the time. But we had purpose.

The Balancing Act

Every day felt like a test. A new responsibility. A new bill. A new reminder that we had dug ourselves into a pit so deep that light seemed far above.

Debts were stacked like walls around us personal loans, bank loans, borrowed help and yet, the money in our hands was barely enough for milk and travel. After long conversations and nights of quiet thinking, we decided: one of us would stay with the baby, and the other would work. It was the only way forward.

We looked at each other and said it without saying it
"Whoever gets the better job, will carry the weight."
And with life's strange ways, I was the one who found work first.

It was a modest job at a nearby office, the salary just enough to spark hope but not silence worry. I remember the first day clearly my hands trembled as I packed my bag. My baby was just over two months old. My body still healing, my heart still stretching between two worlds the one I loved, and the one I needed to survive.

I kissed my son's forehead and whispered,
"Mumma will be back soon, my little warrior."

Dev stood behind me, holding our child, saying nothing just a tight nod. I knew he wanted to say, *"I'm proud of you,"* but emotions don't always find words when life is heavy.

Those first few weeks were chaos. I didn't even have proper travel money some days. I'd wait long for buses, skip meals to save coins, and return home with aching feet and a tired smile, only to hold my baby again that moment was my only healing.

At night, when the baby slept, I'd sit by the window staring at the sky, asking silently,
"Is this really what life has planned for us? So much pain for just a breath of peace?"

But I never gave up.
Because I couldn't.
Because I was a mother now.
Because I had to rise for him.

Evenings became our little sanctuary a quiet, shared rhythm of care and compromise.

While I was away at work, **Dev** turned into a full-time father without hesitation. He would feed the baby, change diapers, rock him gently when he cried, and learn all the delicate nuances of a newborn's world. He would often tell me with a half-smile,
"I never knew I could do all this... but he teaches me every day."

And my mother, despite her illness and Parkinson's, offered what strength she could. She would sit beside the baby, sing old lullabies in her soft, trembling voice, or

keep watch while Dev prepared the meals.
"You go work with peace of mind," she would say. *"I'll
protect this house in my way."*

There were many nights I returned home to see the baby
asleep on Dev's chest, and my mother dozing nearby that
sight stitched my broken spirits back together.

Some days were too heavy. There were moments I would
cry silently while washing baby bottles or cooking late at
night.
*"We'll come out of this. I promise myself. Just need to hold on
a little more."*

"Hold On"

*In the softest corners of struggle and flame,
A mother walked forward with no one to name.
Bills in her hand, and a prayer in her chest,
She worked through the ache, gave her silence some rest.*

*He rocked the baby, while hours went by,
Learning the lull of a midnight sigh.
And the old hands of a mother, frail but true,
Folded peace into chaos, like only she knew.*

*This was no palace, no golden throne,
But it was love, layered in bone.
Hold on they told themselves through the storm,
For one day, dreams would rise and form.*

CHAPTER SEVENTEEN

The Pause That Spoke

The world slowed down.

One by one, shutters rolled down, city lights dimmed, and streets that once echoed with footsteps stood eerily silent. The news was everywhere **COVID-19** had gripped the world in its fist. For many, it was panic. For us, it was both a fear and ironically a momentary sigh of relief.

The government declared a temporary hold on loan recoveries. Banks and creditors were instructed not to press for EMIs or debts. It felt like a small crack of light had entered a room long shrouded in darkness. The mountain of pressure on our shoulders didn't vanish, but at least it paused.

At home, I looked around a little baby wrapped in warmth, completely unaware of the chaos outside, and **my mother**, fragile and aging, requiring continuous care. Fear and hope wrestled inside me daily. What if the virus entered our home? What if we lost everything we were just beginning to rebuild?

But I didn't let fear take root. With sanitizers, masks, careful steps, and stronger prayers, we navigated the days. My job my one lifeline remained. I was lucky. Remote work became my savior.

I worked from home, tapping away on the keyboard while my baby napped beside me and my mother watched quietly from her corner. Life had never been this complex, yet never this intimate. After a few months, I resumed work at the office, masked and guarded, but thankful. Every month's salary was a blessing a promise that we'd survive one more cycle of bills, milk powder, medicines, and loan repayments.

I saw the world shift. People lost jobs, homes, and even loved ones. And yet, we held on not because we had it easy, but because we simply refused to give up.

During this time, I finally made peace with something that had haunted me: the failed business. I shut it down for good. Letting it go wasn't a loss it was a liberation. That chapter had given us only burdens, not hope. And I wasn't ready to carry one more burden. Not when my hands were already full of responsibilities and dreams.

Every night, I watched my son sleep, his chest rising and falling gently, and felt the silent whisper of grace. Despite the storms, God had stayed beside us from days of empty pockets and sleepless nights to now, where even amid a pandemic, we were standing.

From no house to a home,
From no job to security,
From uncertainty to resilience...

The path hasn't been easy, but it's ours. And as the world slowly began to reopen, so did a small door in my heart—to new hopes, new dreams, and the belief that this life, however imperfect, is still full of possibilities.

How many storms can a single heart weather before it breaks?
And yet, here I am still standing. Still breathing. Still believing.

Sometimes, I wonder if life was testing me or preparing me.

Maybe both.

I've learned that strength doesn't always roar
sometimes it's the whisper at midnight, telling you to hold on just one more day.

Every unpaid bill, every tear, every late-night prayer,
they've stitched me into someone I never imagined I could become.

Not perfect, but powerful. Not fearless, but fiercely hopeful.

I used to think survival meant scraping through.
Now I know it means *choosing* to smile, even when everything inside you trembles.

In the silence of this home, in the softness of my child's breath,
in the tired eyes of my mother there's a kind of peace money can't buy.

No matter what comes next, I'll walk into it with open arms.
Because this life, with all its mess and miracles, is still mine.
And quietly, steadily...

We rise.

CHAPTER EIGHTEEN

A House That Hummed with Peace

The boxes were lighter this time.

Not because we had fewer things, but because we had lighter hearts.

Slowly and steadily, we had started repaying the debts — not just the ones owed to banks and lenders, but the invisible ones too... the debts of sleepless nights, unspoken prayers, quiet endurance. It wasn't over, but we were walking on firmer ground.

The new house was rented, yes but to me, it felt earned. A small space, but I saw it with eyes of gratitude. I imagined where the curtains would hang, how the cushions would add warmth, and how the soft glow of the evening light would wrap our little home in peace. I wanted it to breathe harmony to be a place where my child would grow up feeling safe, where my mother would feel comforted, and where we would rediscover each other as a couple.

"You always see the home before the walls are painted," Dev smiled one evening, watching me place a small plant by the window.

"Because I dream in colors only peace can paint," I replied softly.

We bought second-hand pieces a lamp here, a rug there not perfect, but personal. Each item had its place and its reason. Just like us imperfect, but strong.

There was still very little money left at the end of the month. But now, I had started finding contentment in small joys:

My son's giggles when he ran barefoot across the hall.

The smell of my mother's homemade food filling the house.

A quiet moment on the balcony with Dev, sipping tea and saying nothing.

In between survival, I was now learning how to live.

CHAPTER NINETEEN

The Storm Before the Stillness

It started with silence.

Not the comforting kind but the one that fills the house like fog, seeping into corners, making everything feel colder than it is.

Dev and I had been off not arguing exactly, but not connecting either. Misunderstandings layered like thin sheets of ice: one comment here, one oversight there. It was nothing explosive, just... distance. And distance has a way of making you doubt what was once certain.

One evening, while folding laundry, I said sharply, "It's always me adjusting always me figuring things out while you..."

He cut in, tiredly, "And it's always me being blamed for everything."

The words cracked open something that had been building. There were raised voices, watery eyes, accusations masked as questions.

"Do you even see what I'm going through?"

"Do you even ask how I'm doing?"

That night, we went to bed facing opposite walls.

But here's what the years of struggle had taught us: *storms don't always break things sometimes they shake loose what needs healing.*

The next morning, I went out for a walk alone. The sky was just waking up. The stillness reminded me of something I had forgotten: peace doesn't always come from others sometimes, it has to rise from within.

That's when I began the journey inward.

I found an online course on healing and energy work. Then another, on basic astrology. Something about these ancient practices pulled me gently inward — like a whisper from the universe I had been too busy to hear before.

With each lesson, I found clarity.

With each meditation, I softened.

One evening, after weeks of slowly finding my center again, I sat beside Dev and said, "I've been changing not because of you, but because I had to find myself again. And maybe we lost each other for a while, but I want to find *us* again too."

He didn't respond with big words. He just held my hand and said,

"Even in the dark, I knew we'd find the light."

Yes, others had tried to interfere.

Yes, there were moments when love felt like a tired old scarf faded, frayed.

But we had been through too much. Struggled too much. Loved too deeply.

Maybe it wasn't destiny. Maybe it was just two people refusing to let go.

And maybe... that was enough.

The Storm Before the Stillness (Extended)

It was subtle at first missed words, quiet sighs, side glances. But over time, the space between us thickened.

Dev and I, once inseparable in our shared struggles, were beginning to drift under the weight of daily survival. Tensions rose not because we didn't care, but because we cared too much and didn't know how to express it anymore.

One night, after a long day of juggling work, our son, and endless bills, I snapped.

"You don't understand me anymore," I said, standing by the kitchen sink, my back turned.

Dev replied, his voice low but sharp, "And you've stopped seeing me too. You're not the only one carrying weight here."

That night, we barely spoke. Just the soft hum of the fan above and our thoughts racing in silence.

Days passed like this quiet but heavy. I cried in the shower, asking the universe, *why is love so hard, even after surviving so much?*

One morning, while scrolling through my phone at 3 AM, I came across a webinar on energy healing. I hesitated... but something inside nudged me to register. That single click changed something in me.

I started learning **Reiki healing**, **chakra balancing**, and the ancient wisdom of **astrology**. I didn't even tell Dev at first—I just dived into it. For the first time in years, I was doing something purely for myself.

"I'm doing a course," I told him one evening over tea.

He raised an eyebrow. "Another job?"

"No," I smiled faintly. "A job for the soul."

As the weeks passed, I found myself waking early not to finish chores, but to meditate, journal, and study. I learned how trauma lives in the body, how thoughts carry energy, how everything every struggle has a reason. The knowledge healed something ancient in me. It felt like I was finally sweeping the dust off parts of my spirit I had long abandoned.

Dev noticed the change.

"You seem... calmer," he said one night as we folded clothes side by side.

"I'm learning to breathe through pain instead of breaking in it," I replied softly.

We sat in silence. Not the old, bitter one but a warm, comforting quiet that said *I see you. I'm still here.*

One weekend, I shared a small healing session with Dev. Just placing my hands gently over his shoulders, inviting peace in.

He closed his eyes, and whispered, "It's like you've become light."

"No," I said, smiling. "I've just started finding the light inside me."

That journey my *path of healing* saved me in more ways than I can count. It reminded me who I was before life hardened me. It showed me that even in the most broken moments, we are always capable of growth. Of softness. Of love.

Yes, we had arguments. Misunderstandings. Even moments when I wondered if our roads were diverging.

But something stronger always pulled us back.

Maybe it was our shared history. Maybe it was the battles we survived.

Or maybe it was simply this: we still chose each other.

CHAPTER TWENTY

A New Light Within

The days moved on like waves some calm, some crashing, but all pulling us forward. After so many years of struggle, we had reached a point where survival wasn't the only goal. Slowly, a shift was happening inside me.

Our home, though modest and rented, was a canvas I began to paint with peace. I placed small plants in the windows, lit soft lamps in corners, and hung meaningful words on the walls mantras of hope and strength. The rooms began to reflect what I felt inside: a quiet, growing strength.

One day, while sitting alone on the balcony with my notebook and a warm cup of tea, I felt a deep pull. It wasn't about work, finances, or responsibilities. It was something more—something spiritual. The years had carved their lessons into my bones. And now, something inside whispered, *"Now is the time to heal, not just survive."*

I started reading, listening, exploring paths that spoke to my soul Reiki, crystal healing, meditation, astrology. It was like a door opened to a world I had always sensed but never dared to step into. I enrolled in an online healing course a small step, but it felt like reclaiming something that was always mine.

The lessons weren't just about chakras or stars. They were about *me*. About my pain, my forgiveness, my power. I would light a candle each evening, place my hands on my heart, and repeat the affirmations I learned. I felt peace trickle back into the cracks life had left behind.

Dev was skeptical at first. One evening he said,
"You really think these things work?"
I smiled, *"They're not magic. They're mirrors. They help me see things I didn't want to face before."*
He didn't say anything more, but he never stopped me again.

Our relationship had its dips too. With all that we had gone through loans, betrayals, losses there were times we couldn't hear each other. I remember one night after an argument, I cried silently beside him. We weren't fighting over something big, just small weariness that builds over years.

But the next morning, he made me tea without saying a word. And that was enough. We always came back to each other. That was our way quiet, unspoken love stitched between the days.

One afternoon, when I told Dev about my first paid healing session with a client, he looked at me and said,
"I'm proud of you. You really found something that belongs to you."
That moment meant more than any achievement.

I was no longer just a survivor, a mother, a wife I was becoming a seeker. And slowly, a guide. I still had debts. I still had wounds. But I also had purpose.

And sometimes, that's enough to begin again

CHAPTER TWENTY-ONE

The Power Within

Time, they say, doesn't heal everything but it teaches you how to live with it. And by now, I had learned to carry the past like a sacred bundle. Not as a burden, but as a part of me.

With each passing day, my healing journey grew deeper. The more I learned, the more I realized I had the capacity not just to recover, but to help others. Certification after certification, I studied late into the night while the house slept—my son curled up beside me, Dev reading quietly, my mother humming an old song in the background.

My notebook was filled with chakra diagrams, planetary alignments, and journaling prompts. I had candles of every color and crystals nestled in small bowls across the shelves. What was once a home of pure survival now started glowing with intention and energy.

And then it happened my first real healing breakthrough.

A woman from my building approached me. She had seen me light incense every evening on my balcony and asked, *"Do you do some kind of energy work?"*

I hesitated, but I said yes.

She broke down. Her story poured out relationship struggles, health issues, and mental fatigue. I listened. For the first time, I wasn't just a daughter, a wife, or a mother. I was a healer. I offered her a session. I used what I had learned—Reiki, intention setting, aura clearing.

The next day, she called to say, *"I felt something shift inside me. Lighter. Calmer. I slept after weeks."*

That moment rewrote something inside me. I had never felt more certain of my path.

Still, Dev and I were not always on the same page. There were times we argued not out of lack of love, but due to stress, exhaustion, and unspoken needs. Sometimes his silence hurt. Sometimes my emotions were too loud. But in the middle of all the tension, we never walked away from each other. Our foundation had been built in fire, and it held.

One night, after an emotional disagreement, I sat by the window, holding my healing journal. Tears quietly rolled down my cheeks. Dev walked in, unsure, awkward. He sat beside me and held my hand not with words, but with presence.

"Maybe this is also healing," I whispered, *"Learning to forgive even when nothing is said."*

He nodded. That was our strength resilience in silence, forgiveness in gestures.

As days passed, I continued learning tarot, astrology, energy balancing. Every client I helped, every chart I read, brought me closer to who I was meant to be.

This chapter of life wasn't about escaping the past it was about alchemizing it into light. I realized healing isn't a destination. It's a way of walking through life.

And even in a world full of brokenness, I had found my medicine.

CHAPTER TWENTY-TWO

A Promise Made in Quiet Light

Today, as we sat quietly on the balcony just the two of us, the world softened by the golden hue of the setting sun I felt the gentle pull of memories.

No grand celebration. No lavish cake. Just a homemade one, whipped together with what we had. But somehow, it felt like more than enough.

We looked at each other with tired but content eyes. In that silence, we both were speaking. Recalling those countless days when we didn't even have enough to buy a meal outside, when we counted coins to refill gas or stretch groceries for a week. The days when unpaid bills sat like silent guests on the corner table, and our dreams seemed just out of reach.

"Do you remember," I said softly, "that birthday when we didn't even have money for a cake?"

Dev smiled, "And still, you lit a candle and sang. That was enough. That always was."

We sat in that stillness, surrounded by the chaos we'd survived. The emotional storms, the broken expectations, the debts that hung heavy. We had seen days where love felt tired, stretched thin by responsibility. And yet, we never gave up not on each other, not on our dreams.

There were moments when silence grew loud between us, when frustration clouded the air. There were days when I questioned everything. Days when we saw the true faces behind masks, when relationships around us revealed cracks. And yet, even in those moments, we clung to our vow—not one we made at a wedding altar, but one made in the kitchen, over broken cups and shared tears: *"We won't give up. We'll stay together through it all."*

That promise carried us.

Every struggle stitched us closer. Every hardship deepened our bond. We were no longer the same people who started this journey, but we had grown with more understanding, more patience, more respect.

On this birthday, we didn't need much. The love we shared was the biggest gift. The small cake baked at home, laughter echoing in our little kitchen, our son giggling, and my mother watching us with quiet blessings in her eyes this was our celebration.

As we clinked cups of homemade tea, Dev looked at me and said, *"Whatever comes next, we'll face it. Together."*

I nodded, my heart full.

And I knew, deep inside, no matter how hard the days may come, this love raw, real, and earned through trials would always be our anchor.

CHAPTER TWENTY-THREE

The Name We Gave, The Love He Became

The days rolled by gently, and our son—our little miracle grew before our eyes.

It was time. Time to give him his name... a name that would carry the legacy of our love, our struggles, our victories, and our silent prayers. A name that would belong to both Dev and Arti, and to the world that had tried to break us but never could.

We sat together one evening, staring at him as he played with an old spoon his favorite toy, ignoring the new ones we'd gathered around him. That was his way. Simple. Content. Observant. A child who smiled with his eyes and lit up the room without a sound.

Choosing his name felt sacred, like carving a blessing into stone. And when we finally spoke it aloud, it felt just right as though the universe had whispered it into our hearts long ago.

He was born into the most difficult of times, yet he brought with him only peace. Not once did he cry endlessly for attention or throw fits for toys. He was gentle, understanding, as if he knew somehow how much we had already endured.

He never brought us struggle. Not financially. Not emotionally. If anything, he brought us relief, a calm rhythm to the chaos of life. It was as if God had listened to every plea, every prayer I had whispered in quiet corners, and sent him as an answer.

I remember watching him nap in my arms, his tiny fingers curled around mine. There was no greater joy. No greater miracle.

As he grew, his independence shone brightly. He was curious, active, affectionate and incredibly sharp. He picked up on emotions quickly, as if his heart had a wisdom beyond his years. And with each passing day, he made our home brighter, our burdens lighter.

His first birthday arrived during the time when the world was still holding its breath the era of COVID. No parties, no guests, no grand gatherings. But our hearts were full.

We decorated the house with what little we had. Balloons in corners, ribbons on the door, and a cake baked at home. It wasn't about grandeur it was about grace.

Our loved ones joined us from their screens, smiling through pixelated video calls, singing birthday songs from afar. And yet, the warmth reached us. It felt like he was surrounded by a thousand arms of love, even in distance.

As we sang and clapped, I caught Dev's eyes across the room. There was a glimmer there a silent acknowledgment. We had made it. We had brought this beautiful soul into the world and nurtured him through its storms.

And as I held our son close that night, whispering his name softly in his ear, I thanked the stars above for sending us a child who taught us more about life in a year than we had learned in decades.

Our world fragile, hopeful, unfinished felt complete with him.

CHAPTER TWENTY-FOUR

Little Steps, Giant Leaps

We had initially planned to put him in nursery, but life as always nudged us in another direction. With my mother unable to travel and finances still tightly bound, we made a decision that felt both practical and hopeful: to directly enroll him into Montessori Level 2 at a dear friend's preschool.

It felt like a small step at the time, but it turned out to be one of the most beautiful leaps in our parenting journey.

Every day, our little one came home with stories—tiny, magical windows into his world. "Today, I helped my friend," he would say with a sparkle in his eyes. Or sometimes, "Teacher gave me a star!" That gentle voice of his, so soft and filled with sweetness, carried so much purity and emotion. His words came out clear, his thoughts even clearer. We often paused and looked at each other in disbelief how can someone so small be so articulate, so aware?

Watching him mingle with other children, learning to share, to speak, to respond with empathy it filled our hearts with silent pride. He wasn't just growing physically; he was unfolding like a flower, one petal at a time.

Each evening became a celebration of his drawings, his songs, the new words he learned in different languages. We used to sit together, Dev and I, quietly absorbing the joy our child brought into our lives. We saw glimpses of our love, our values, and maybe even our dreams reflected in him.

We had faced storms, tides, and heartbreaks. But this... this was calm. This was our reward.

And through it all, we never stopped thanking God. His grace had carried us when our legs couldn't. He gave us strength when we were weak, light when we were lost and this child, this gentle soul, as a divine reminder that we were never alone.

CHAPTER TWENTY-FIVE

The Healer Within

It didn't happen overnight. The journey from emotional chaos to spiritual calm was slow, painful, and yet utterly magical.

There was a time when I couldn't even sit still. My thoughts were like a thousand tabs open at once: finances, responsibilities, motherhood, loss, frustration. Every night, I would lie in bed with a heavy chest and a restless heart.

One day, as if guided by something unseen, I stumbled upon a short workshop on energy healing. "Reiki Level 1 – Self-Healing Begins Within." I don't know what pushed me to sign up, but something in me whispered, *try.*

The first time I felt energy in my hands real, warm, pulsating I cried.

It was like meeting myself for the first time. The pain, the numbness, the wounds that were buried deep inside… started surfacing. I was not just learning healing I was healing myself.

And then the stories began.

There was a neighbor's child, constantly ill despite medication. I offered a short healing session. The next day, the fever broke. The mother hugged me and cried, saying, *"I don't know what you did, but thank you."*

Another time, Dev was restless and anxious. Work wasn't going well, and he was barely sleeping. I placed my hands gently on his forehead and chanted what I had learned. That night, for the first time in weeks, he slept like a child. When he woke up, he looked at me in wonder, *"What did you do?"* he asked.

I smiled, *"I didn't do anything. It was the energy. I'm just the medium."*

With time, I studied further Reiki advanced levels, Angel Healing, Chakra Cleansing, Tarot, Astrology. Every certificate didn't just decorate my wall it became a new doorway to light, to helping others, to finding lost pieces of myself.

Soon, people started coming. Friends of friends. Women with emotional trauma. Couples seeking clarity. Teenagers facing anxiety. I became a listener, a guide, and a channel.

Some came to me shattered, and left with tears of peace.

There was one young woman, on the verge of divorce. After three healing sessions and simple guided meditations, she said, "I feel like I've returned home to myself."

That sentence became the theme of my journey: returning home to oneself.

I still cooked, cleaned, did laundry, and looked after my family but something in me had shifted. My home was no longer just four walls. It was a healing space. My hands were no longer just hands; they carried warmth. My voice became prayer. My silence became presence.

And through it all, Dev watched. At first with curiosity, then awe, and finally pride. "You were born for this," he once said. "You turn pain into power."

Maybe I was. Maybe the darkness I endured was the cocoon I needed.

Because now, when people ask me what I do, I don't say I'm just a healer.

I say **"I help people remember who they are... by first remembering who I am."**

CHAPTER TWENTY-SIX

The Whisper of Shiva, My Param Pita

My healing journey didn't just stop with certificates or successful healing sessions. It evolved—into something deeper, something sacred, something profoundly personal.

It became *me*.

There were days when I was my own patient. When my own thoughts screamed louder than the world outside. When the silence at night felt heavier than the burdens I carried. But in those moments when I thought I was utterly alone I felt Him.

Shiva. My Param Pita.

Not just a deity on the wall or a chant in my prayer, but a presence. A stillness. A knowing.

He didn't appear in grand miracles. He showed up in the quiet strength that returned to me after every emotional storm. He was in the voice that said, *"You are not alone. You never were."*

Through Him, I began to walk the inner path of purification, truth, and surrender.

No, I won't say I've become fearless. That would be a lie. I am human. And to be human is to feel everything—the joy, the sorrow, the fear, the anger. Especially in a world where people wear so many masks, where truth is often buried under layers of convenience.

But somewhere along the way, I developed an inner clarity.

A quiet power that doesn't need to expose others, or prove myself to anyone. I see. I sense. I know. But I keep it within. I choose peace over reaction, stillness over drama. That is the growth my healing brought me.

Today, when I look in the mirror, I don't see just a woman who went through storms. I see a woman who dances in the rain now.

I have faith in my becoming.

I know I will reach where I'm destined to be—not because success will chase me, but because success is already walking beside me, quietly, patiently, like a shadow.

We live in a rental house today. It's small, simple, yet full of warmth and dreams. But every single corner of this space knows the vision we hold as a family:

A home.

Not just bricks and walls, but a *dream bungalow* where my mother will have her own peaceful room on the ground floor. A living room filled with light and laughter, an open kitchen where aromas carry stories, and a dining space where gratitude is served daily. Each floor reflecting a part of us our style, our vision, our journey.

I see it. So clearly.

Sometimes Dev and I sit, smile, and describe every detail of that dream home. We talk about wall textures, balcony views, garden corners, the room where our child will grow with joy and books and music. And I know it's not just a wish. It's a certainty.

Because Shiva walks with us.

Because love still lives in our togetherness.

And because healing once started never truly ends.

It expands.

And so do we.

And so, I continue walking this path with Shiva by my side, with my family in my heart, and with my dreams in my eyes.

Every step may not be easy, but it is sacred.

"When the world whispers doubt, let your soul echo with faith. For those who walk with truth, the path may be silent but never lonely." - disha...!

This is not the end.

This is the becoming.

CHAPTER TWENTY-SEVEN

Living the Everyday – With Dignity, Dreams & Devotion

Every family, behind their doors and smiles, carries a world of responsibilities, challenges, unspoken struggles, and silent victories. It's not always about big events but the day-to-day chaos, the decisions made in silence, the bills, the balancing acts, and the invisible work that holds a home together.

We were no different.

Like many, we had dreams tucked away quietly between utility bills and grocery lists. From managing expenses to trying out small ventures, from Dev taking up odd jobs to me juggling between my healing practice and writing our life was never a straight path. We didn't have shortcuts. What we had was **courage,** and **a refusal to take the easy way out.**

There were days when Dev and I would sit late into the night discussing our next steps what more we could try, how else we could push our limits without losing ourselves. We tried multiple things: freelance work, part-time jobs, skill upgrades... you name it. Not everything worked. But every failure taught us where not to fall again.

What kept us grounded wasn't just necessity it was dignity.

We never wanted to grow by stepping over someone else's efforts or by compromising our values. Even when people around us seemed to take the easier, faster roads—ours was slow, uncertain, but **true**. And today, even if we are still building our foundation, we know it's strong. It's ours.

As a healer, I found that life is not always about changing what's outside—it's about transforming what's within. Through this lens, I began to understand people deeper, not just from their words, but from the energy they carried. I could feel their burdens, just as I had carried mine.

Many came to me not just as clients, but as souls seeking hope. And all I wanted was to be that light for them, even if for a moment. I often prayed not just for myself and my family, but for them too. For all those who trust me with their pain.

"I see you, I hear you, and I pray for you."

That became a silent mantra I lived with.

Even today, I close my eyes sometimes and visualize a life that's waiting to bloom our dream home, where my mother has her peaceful corner, where my son runs freely, and where Dev and I look back with a smile, knowing we lived with grace.

I believe we will get there. Because we're walking with truth, and that's the only fuel we need.

"Your dreams don't need shortcuts. They need belief, dignity, and the courage to walk slowly—but never stop." -**disha**

Every family carries its own rhythm of struggle and survival. And in our home, that rhythm often sounded like whispered prayers, small sacrifices, big dreams, and the constant pulse of "don't give up." There were bills. There were long days. But we kept choosing hard work, dignity, and honesty over shortcuts.

We knew success wasn't going to knock on our door—we had to build the door first.

While Dev and I tried our hands at various jobs, failed business ventures, and part-time gigs just to keep the lights on, I also found my heart pulling me in another direction—a quieter, deeper path.

CHAPTER TWENTY-EIGHT

Healing.

It wasn't something I planned, it found me. I began exploring energy work, studying ancient sciences, diving into astrology, and slowly, learning the true meaning of inner awareness. I wasn't just reading theories I was living through transformations, both within myself and in others.

One day, I remember, a young man came to me completely shattered. You could see it in his eyes; his soul was tired. He sat across from me and said, *"I have many things I've never spoken to anyone... but something about you makes me feel like I can."*

He went on to share stories filled with guilt, regret, heartbreak, and grief. The kind of emotional weight that can quietly destroy a person from the inside. I didn't interrupt him I simply listened.

When he was done, he looked up with tears in his eyes and said,

"I don't know why... but I feel like something inside me just healed."

In that moment, I knew it wasn't me. It was the Universe. The divine. The energy flowing through me as a channel. I was just a medium. And I felt humbled, not proud. Humbled that God chose me to be part of someone's healing journey.

That wasn't the only moment. Each person who walks into my space for healing, I treat as a soul sent by the divine. I don't offer miracles. I offer presence, prayer, methods, and unwavering intent that they find their light.

"If someone asks me today, 'Who are you?'—I now have my answer.

I am a passionate healer.

I am a writer with a fire in my heart.

And I have a goal—to build my identity, earn fame and fortune not just for myself, but to uplift others, and make my extended family proud of the name I leave behind."

CHAPTER TWENTY-NINE

Bhavati – The Voice Within Every Woman

They say every writer has a book that writes *them* back a book so close to the heart that it feels like breathing life into pages. *Bhavati* is that book for me.

This is my third book. My first one was a love story written in poems a journey filled with emotions, uncertainties, and endless delays. I was clueless back then about how I would publish it. With limited resources, no guidance, and only hope in my heart, I still dared to dream. I carved my own way, one day at a time, writing late into nights, between chores, responsibilities, and silence.

The second book was another long journey. Scattered writings on random papers, in diaries, saved drafts collected over the years like fragments of my own soul. It took me time and patience to pull them together and shape them into a book. I never rushed. I always believed, *"If it's not my best version yet, I won't speak of it. Let my words do justice first."* I didn't do heavy marketing. I let the books live quietly, like seeds planted deep, waiting for the right season to bloom.

But *Bhavati* this was different.

Bhavati came to life through the voices of women I met. Some were friends. Some strangers. Some were hesitant. Some broken. Some still gathering the strength to even tell their stories. I met them not as a healer or a writer, but as a woman who could *listen without judgment*. I earned their trust. I gave them space. I became their mirror.

Each story shook something within me. While they thought I was giving them a voice, the truth was—they were giving me mine. Their pain, their strength, their silence it filled pages. Their stories reminded me that for every one woman I met, there are millions more whose stories are lost, buried, silenced.

For a while, that thought made me feel helpless—*what can I do alone in this big world?* But then, a deeper voice within me said, *"You're not alone. You're doing your part. And that is enough."*

I may not have a global platform yet. I may not have big publishers chasing me. But I have *truth*. I have *intention*. And I have *Bhavati*. A book that I hope will touch the hearts of many women young, old, wounded, silent and help them feel seen, heard, and valued.

This book isn't just stories. It's a reflection. A tribute. A voice.
It is a *gift* from one woman to another. From *me* to *us all*.

"When one woman shares her story, she heals.

When another woman reads it, she awakens.

And when many rise together—truth becomes power." -
disha

CHAPTER THIRTY

The Unexpected Blessing

Life was moving forward slowly but surely. Every day brought a new thought, a new plan what else could we do to build a stable life for our family? Dev and I often sat after Shivaay slept, just talking, sometimes in silence and sometimes with dreams spilling into the night.

That evening was one of those peaceful ones. The sky was quiet, our hearts a little lighter. We sat with tea in hand, our backs resting against the wall, legs stretched out on the floor.

"Dev," I said softly, "have you ever thought what we'd do if Roshan returned our money?"

He chuckled, "Every now and then. Then I quickly shut that door in my head. It hurts less that way."

I looked at him, "But just imagine... if we had that money, we could start again... maybe finally think about that house, or clearing off the rest of the debts."

He nodded, eyes lost in thought. "One day, Arti. One day we will. That money might or might not return, but our karma always does."

We spoke for hours that night, floating between what-ifs and maybes, until sleep took over our tired bodies.

The next morning, as we sat at the breakfast table, Dev's phone rang. He answered casually, chewing the last bite of his toast. But as the person spoke on the other end, I saw his expression change—his eyes widened, his back straightened, and his mouth opened slightly in disbelief.

"Hello?... Yes?... Are you sure? Wait—can you just repeat that once again?"

I looked at him, confused. "What happened?"

He didn't answer right away. He was typing something on his phone, his fingers trembling. Then, after a pause, he looked up at me, barely able to speak.

"We got it."

"Got what?" I asked, my heart beating faster.

He simply turned his phone screen toward me.

"XXXXXXX amount credited in your account."

I gasped. "Dev... is this real?"

He nodded slowly. "Roshan returned the money. After all these years... it's here. It's really here."

Tears welled up in both our eyes. I reached for his hand. We just sat there, frozen in that beautiful moment, overwhelmed.

"Mom!" I called out. "We got our money back! Roshan returned it!"

She came out of the kitchen, wiping her hands on her saree. "What are you saying?"

Dev repeated, "We finally got it back, Ma. Look..."

We lit a small diya, folded our hands, and offered our gratitude.

"Thank you, Shiva," I whispered, "Thank you for always watching over us."

We hugged tightly three hearts finally breathing a little easier.

That morning, we sat back down and started planning.

"We can put some of this aside," Dev said. "The house dream—it's closer now."

"And Shivaay's school. Maybe we can get him some better books and enroll him for activities."

"And...," he looked at me, "maybe... your healing space? That dream you always had?"

I smiled, wiping my tears. "Yes. It's time."

"Sometimes, the blessings we wait for arrive when we're just about to stop expecting. And in that moment, we learn—faith was never foolish. It was divine timing in disguise."

CHAPTER THIRTY-ONE

From Silence to Strength

As I sat alone that evening, after the chaos of the day had settled, I held a warm cup of tea and looked out at the sky slowly turning orange. I could still feel the vibration of that moment the moment we saw the message, the moment our hearts skipped a beat, and then melted into tears.

How long had we waited for this day? Not just for the money... but for justice. For closure. For that breath of relief, we had forgotten we were holding.

I remembered the countless nights we both silently cried on our pillows so the other wouldn't hear... the heavy days where we didn't even have words to speak, just small smiles and tired hope to get us through. Yet we never gave up.

That's what love does. That's what struggle teaches you. To hold on. To believe.

Looking at Dev today, his face lit up like I hadn't seen in years. He deserved this. We both did.

A voice inside me whispered, *"This is only the beginning."* And I believed it. Because this time, the beginning wasn't built on just hope—it was built on proof that the universe was listening. It always had been.

I whispered softly to myself:

"I have walked through fire and came out with light.

I have been broken, yet I chose to heal.

I have waited, and today, my wait found its meaning."

As a healer, I always told others to trust. As Arti the woman, the wife, the mother I finally saw that my own trust had not been in vain.

We are not just building a house we are building a life. We are not just dreaming we are living those dreams, brick by brick.

And now... it's time to rise higher.

CHAPTER THIRTY-TWO

A Leap of Faith

The morning sunlight streamed into our home as I sipped my tea and looked at Dev. We had a long discussion the previous night, one that felt both exciting and scary. The money we received was a blessing, but not enough to book a house—yet it was enough to make a move. The kind of move that could open new doors.

"Let's not rush into anything big," Dev said thoughtfully. "But what if we use it wisely for protection and growth?"

We nodded in agreement and chose to invest in something we had postponed for years **insurance** for ourselves and our child. It felt like finally taking responsibility for our future. Then, quietly, I shared what had been on my heart for a while.

"Dev... what if I rent a small space for my healing and tarot practice?"

There was silence for a moment.

"Are you sure?" he asked, reading the concern behind my smile. "It's an investment and once it's gone, it's gone."

That night, I lit a diya in front of Shiva, my Parampita. I closed my eyes, surrendered my fear, and prayed, asking the Universe for guidance. During the silence, I felt something shift within me an energy, an answer. A quiet but strong **"Yes."**

With that faith, we went ahead and rented a small office space. It wasn't fancy. But it was mine. My sacred space.

At first, I was nervous. What if no one came? What if I failed? But soon, appointments started to flow in—one after the other. The days turned into weeks, and I had no time to spare. The diary was full, the website bookings nonstop.

"Ma'am, how do you manage all this?" one client asked after a session.

I smiled. **"I plan what I can... and the rest is taken care of by Him,"** I replied, pointing upwards.

Eventually, I realized I needed help. I reached out to one of my students—an angelic soul, deeply connected to healing herself.

"Would you like to manage my office bookings and appointments?" I asked over a call.

"From your home, at your comfort. I just need someone trustworthy," I added.

She was surprised, touched, and agreed instantly. I discussed everything with her her work, the stipend, and our mutual goals. Handing her the responsibility felt like lifting a huge weight off my shoulders.

One Monday morning, just as I was getting ready, my son ran from the bedroom and wrapped his tiny arms around me.

"Mumma, yay! Today you're not going to the office!"

His joy struck something deep inside me. I looked at his innocent face, so full of love and hope. I made a quick decision.

"Okay, baby. Today I'll go a little late. Let's have breakfast together first."

We laughed, ate, and shared small moments that felt bigger than anything in the world.

Later, I gently told him, "Mumma needs to go to work for a little while, okay? But we'll meet at the healing center soon after."

He nodded with a smile, **"Okay, Mumma."**

That moment, I knew he understood more than most grown-ups ever could.

Days passed. The healing office became a hub of energy, love, and transformation. Then, nearly a year after opening it, something inside me shifted again.

I sat quietly and reflected. The balance between job and passion had worked well... but I was now ready to choose fully.

It was time.

Time to leave my job and step entirely into my soul's work. I had waited for this moment for years—not with impatience, but with determination. The transition wasn't sudden; it was sacred. Guided.

"When your purpose calls louder than your fears, that's when you begin to truly live."

CHAPTER THIRTY-THREE

Planting the Seed of Our Dream

The days had begun to change like seasons shifting gently but surely. The winds around us carried new hopes, and every sunrise felt like another brick placed in the foundation of our dreams.

After nearly a year of nurturing our healing center, Dev and I found ourselves standing on stronger ground—financially, emotionally, and spiritually.

One evening, over our usual cup of tea, Dev looked at me and said with a soft but determined tone:

"I think we're really getting somewhere, Arti. You've built something that people trust. And I... I'm proud of you."

His words meant everything. I reached across the table, smiling.

"It's *we*, Dev. This is ours. Every step, every struggle, every prayer... you've stood beside me."

We had made a major decision recently Dev would continue his job to keep our monthly foundation secure, and I, after years of balancing roles, had finally **quit my** full-time job to dedicate myself completely to my soul work. It was a leap of faith, but one I took with conviction.

Within just four months of opening the office, we had managed to buy our first car a milestone that once seemed like a distant dream. I still remember the way our son Shivaay jumped up and down with joy when he saw the car in the parking lot.

"Mumma, is this ours? Really ours?" he had squealed.

"Yes, baby. Our very first car," I said, lifting him into my arms.

By the grace of Shiva, the blessings of my mother, and the energy of every client who walked into my healing room with faith, we had now built a loyal chain of clients. People who trusted me not just as a healer, but as someone who understood them deeply.

Mary, the young girl I had appointed as my manager, continued to shine. She wasn't working for the money; she worked because she believed in the purpose.

"Di," she once said, "this isn't just a job. I feel like I'm part of something bigger."

And she was. Her dedication, compassion, and quiet strength had become one of the pillars of my practice.

That night, after a long and fulfilling day, Dev and I sat side by side on the couch. The soft hum of silence surrounded us as we both looked at each other with a kind of knowing.

"Let's go see that plot tomorrow," Dev said casually, but I could feel the spark in his voice.

I turned to him, eyes wide.

"Are you serious? You mean *the* plot?"

"Yes," he nodded. "March 22nd. The realtor confirmed. I think it's time, Arti. Time to take the next step."

That night, sleep didn't come easily not because of worry, but because of excitement. The kind that wraps around your heart like a whisper of dreams coming true.

As I lay next to Dev, eyes open in the dark, I whispered a prayer:

"Thank you, God. For showing us light in places we once feared darkness."

"Dreams are never built in a day. But if you build one brick with belief, and another with effort, one day, you'll have a homemade of faith. Today, I see us getting there."

"The journey of a thousand miles begins not with a single step, but with the courage to take it."

In whispered prayers and candlelight,
We built our dreams from silent night.
Not all at once, but slow and true,
With every tear, the heavens knew.

A car, a key, a healing space,
Each step a mark of silent grace.
With faith, we dared to let fears go,
And watched the roots of vision grow.

March wind carried plans we made,
To plant our dreams where hopes don't fade.
With love as seed and work as rain,
We'll build our home, through joy and strain.

CHAPTER THIRTY-FOUR

The Turning of the Tide

It was a calm morning, one that didn't carry the weight of uncertainty anymore, but the freshness of a new beginning. March 22nd had finally arrived the day Dev and I had marked on our calendar not just as a date, but as a symbol of everything we had strived for. The plot visit wasn't just a step it was the threshold of a life we had only dared to imagine during our hardest days.

As we drove to meet the realtor, I held Dev's hand and looked out at the roads, the trees, the sky and I saw everything differently. These weren't just streets anymore. They were roads we had paved with our prayers, tears, healing, and deep love. I looked at Dev, and I didn't just see my husband I saw my co-warrior, my anchor, my mirror.

"Do you remember," I whispered, "how we used to dream of this day while counting coins for groceries?"

He smiled. "I never stopped believing. I just needed to see your eyes every time I doubted."

The plot we saw wasn't just a piece of land. It was the canvas our souls had painted for years. We stood silently, letting our hearts fill it with visions of my mother's ground-floor room, of Shivaay playing in the garden, of meals cooked in our open kitchen, and of laughter echoing through walls that knew our story.

And as if the universe was waiting for our final yes, within one year of that visit, our home stood tall our dream turned reality.

We shifted into our bungalow, a two-floor sanctuary filled with light, life, and love. Each corner reflected a part of us. The open kitchen merged into a warm dining and living space where we shared meals and memories. The garden welcomed morning prayers and evening teas. Every room was a world of comfort, painted in hues that matched our energies—soft pastels that calmed, warm earth tones that grounded.

The bathrooms were luxurious, with bathtubs for long healing soaks, and every corner of the home was adorned with interiors we had once only discussed in whispers. The house was equipped with smart technology, blending modern convenience with soulful design. Our black car, once parked in rental spaces, now stood proudly in its own driveway.

And the most fulfilling moment? Watching my mother's eyes shine with peace. Her dream of living in her own home had come true. She walked into her room, placed her hand on the wall, and whispered, "My home... finally."

Our son, Shivaay, now almost six, ran freely through the house, his laughter filling spaces we had built brick by brick with hope. The healing office was flourishing. Dev's stability at work had only strengthened. And I after years of juggling and hustling was now living my passion full-time, helping others find their light, just as I had once sought mine.

That night, sitting in our balcony under the open sky, we didn't need fireworks. Just silence. Just breath. Just love.

Dev looked at me, a gentle smile on his face.

"We're here, Arti. We made it."

I nodded, eyes glistening.

"And this time, we're "In the house we built with faith, every wall echoes our resilience. Every light is a blessing. And every breath is a celebration of the dream we never gave up on." not just surviving. We're living... fully and truly."

It took **a** decade to arrive here. A journey through struggle, faith, healing, betrayal, love, loss, and grace. But here we were—at last. Home.

Epilogue: And So, We Rose...

As the sun set beyond our new home, and laughter echoed through its freshly painted walls, a gentle silence wrapped around us like a warm embrace. For the first time in years, there were no immediate battles to fight, no debts to repay, no dark clouds hovering. We were finally standing on ground we had dreamed of and built with our own hands and hearts.

But life... it never stops evolving.

This may be the end of one journey, but it is just the beginning of another. As Arti steps deeper into her purpose as a healer and author, as Dev continues his own journey of growth, and as little Shivaay blossoms into a curious soul ready to embrace the world—there are still many stories waiting to unfold.

New dreams are taking root.

New challenges will rise.

And the fire within us still burns bright, lighting paths yet to be walked.

Because rising once is just the beginning. Rising again and again is what makes a legacy.

We had finally arrived. The home we once whispered about during sleepless nights had turned into reality. Two floors of warmth and meaning, every wall painted in our nature's colors, every corner echoing the prayers and dreams of our past. My mother sat in her favorite armchair by the garden window, a soft smile on her face one that held years of waiting and unwavering hope. Shivaay, now six, ran barefoot through the living room, laughter trailing behind him like sunlight.

Dev parked our black car under the porch of our very own bungalow. He looked at me and said, "We made it, Arti."

And we had. After nearly a decade of rising quietly, holding onto faith, truth, and one another we had arrived.

But life... it never stops unfolding.

Just when we thought the storms had stilled, a new wind began to stir. Something unexpected was about to knock at our door not to shake what we built, but to test how deeply our roots had grown.

The universe had another chapter waiting for us filled with unfamiliar cities, unspoken truths, and paths that would challenge even the strongest parts of our soul.

Our story isn't over yet.
In fact, it's just beginning again...

Life rarely unfolds the way we imagine. It is a quiet journey of small steps, of unseen struggles and silent victories. *Quietly We Rose* is not just a story of hardships endured or dreams chased; it is a testament to the strength within the unwavering courage that blooms when life presses hardest.

Through storms and shadows, we found light. Through loss and uncertainty, we found love and meaning. The path was never easy, but every challenge shaped us, every tear watered our growth, and every moment of resilience added to our strength.

As this chapter closes, a new one begins one of hope, of peace, and of continuing to rise, quietly but powerfully, toward the life we have always dreamed of. May this story remind you that even in the stillness, even in the quietest moments, there is power.

There is light. There is a promise.

And so, quietly, we rose.

About The Author

Disha Y. Bangera is a woman of grace, resilience, and remarkable depth. A healer by calling and a writer by soul, she turned her life's journey filled with love, loss, faith, and quiet triumphs — into a moving story of hope. A certified Reiki Grand Master and yoga mentor, Disha's work reflects a deep connection to healing, emotional truth, and inner strength. **Quietly We Rose** is her debut book, a memoir woven with real memories and raw reflections that illuminate the spirit of survival. She lives in India with her family, guiding others toward self-awareness and inner peace.

Coming Soon.....part Two

To Be Continued...
Part Two:
Quietly We Rise Higher
Coming Soon
Stay Blessed Stay Happy...!